Monkey's Clever Tale

Andrew Fusek Peters

Ilustrated by
Amanda Montgomery-Higham

Child's Play (International) Ltd
Ashworth Rd, Bridgemead, Swindon, SN5 7YD UK
Swindon   Auburn ME   Sydney
Text © 2003 A. Fusek Peters   Illustrations © 2003 Child's Play (International) Ltd

Ameerah Monkey never goes to school!
All day, she swings through the trees
with her younger brothers and sisters,
playing games and being naughty.

In fact, Ameerah Monkey likes nothing better
than MONKEYING about!

One day, Ameerah Monkey was exploring.
As she tumbled through the tops of the trees,
she spied some silver, shimmering far away
in the distance.

As she climbed closer and stared below,
the silver began to roar and twist like a snake!
It was the river, which flowed all the way to the sea.
She wondered what was on the other side.
It would be so exciting to cross the shining river.

But Ameerah was terrified of water....

Down below, Crocodile was wallowing in the mud
on the bank and picking his very sharp teeth.
Crocodiles are monkeys' worst enemies,
but Ameerah was not at all frightened of this one.

She thought and thought, until suddenly,
Ameerah Monkey had a brilliant idea!

She climbed away from the crocodile
and down to the bottom of a big tree.
There, she found some wood,
burned by hunters to black charcoal.
She took a lump of it and began
to dye her tail black.
Then, she tied it around her waist
and walked back towards the crocodile...

"Good day, Mr Crocodile! I hope you are well!"
Ameerah cried with a smile.
"I wonder if you might carry me across the river?"

Crocodile was astonished! Was the monkey mad?
"But Monkey, dear Monkey...you know
that I am your mortal enemy!" he frowned.
"And that I like nothing better for my dinner
than monkey meat!" he added suspiciously.

"Of course you do!" said Ameerah Monkey.
"Now, which bit of me do you like to eat the best?"

"That's easy!" smiled the crocodile.
"Everybody knows that crocodiles love
monkey tails! Yes, Monkey Tail Soup!"
he answered as he licked his lips
and looked closely at Ameerah.
"But, Monkey, where is your tail?"

"Well now, let me see!
But of course, it's Sunday..." said Ameerah.
"Every Saturday, I wash my tail
and leave it hanging on the washing line!
But, if you carry me over the river,
I will go and fetch it for you, and my brother's
and sister's and mother's and father's tails too!"

Crocodile was excited
by the idea of a monkey tail feast.
But just as Ameerah Monkey thought
that her trick was beginning to work,
Crocodile waddled closer to Ameerah
and peered closely at her tail.

"What's that around your waist?"

Ameerah Monkey jumped back in fright and spluttered,
"It's a belt! Have you never seen a belt before,
dear Mr Crocodile?"

Crocodile shook his head.

"I bought it at the market only the other day!
Isn't it smart?"   Ameerah paraded around
the crocodile, showing off her new 'belt'.

Crocodile was impressed.
"Well Monkey, what a lovely promise.
I shall indeed take you across the river!"
he said.

But suddenly, Ameerah Monkey's tail twitched, as monkey tails sometimes do.

"What was that?" cried the crocodile with alarm and great suspicion. "The belt just moved!"

"Yes, yes, yes!" said Ameerah, wearily. "Don't you know it's a magical belt? Honestly, you crocodiles are quite stupid sometimes! I promise to show you the magic when we reach the other side!" And she gave Crocodile a big wink.

Crocodile had the feeling that Ameerah was being very cheeky. But he couldn't wait for his monkey tail feast.

"Climb onto my tail and hold on tight!" he commanded.

With that, Ameerah jumped onto the long, leathery tail, and the crocodile waded into the water.

The river ran fast and strong and silver. It roared like a lion, and Ameerah Monkey was ever so scared.

"There, there, little monkey. I can feel you shivering with fright!" said Crocodile. "Climb a little higher onto my back and you shall be completely safe!"

Ameerah Monkey climbed up Crocodile's back, and nearer Crocodile's sharp, sharp teeth. By now, they were deep in the river. Ameerah looked down at the water rushing by. She shivered again.

"There, there, little monkey, I can feel you shivering with fright!" said Crocodile. "Climb just a little higher up my back and you shall be completely safe!"

Ameerah Monkey climbed further up Crocodile's back, and even nearer Crocodile's sharp, sharp teeth.

By now they were half-way across the river, and the crocodile was swimming with all his might against the current.
The water looked deep and cold. What if she fell off?
She shivered again.

"There, there, little monkey, I can feel you shivering with fright!" said Crocodile. "Climb right up onto my neck and you shall be completely safe!" he smiled.

Ameerah Monkey climbed carefully onto Crocodile's neck,
and even nearer Crocodile's sharp, sharp teeth.
She clung on with all her might!

Oh! They were so near the other side of the river.
She hoped Crocodile wouldn't eat her up before she got away!

She must think of another way to tempt
the greedy beast onto the shore…

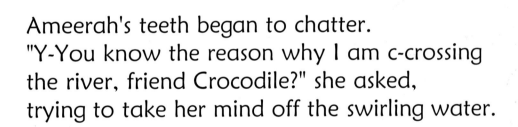

Ameerah's teeth began to chatter.
"Y-You know the reason why I am c-crossing
the river, friend Crocodile?" she asked,
trying to take her mind off the swirling water.

"Yes!" said Crocodile, hungrily.
"To fetch me some monkey tails!"

"E-Exactly!" said Ameerah Monkey.
"But I must also pay for my brand new belt!"
she explained. "You see, on the other side
of the river there is the Opposite Bank!
And that is where I keep all my money - to pay
for food and clothes and other important things!"

Crocodile wondered what the Opposite Bank looked like...

"Anyway!" continued Ameerah,
"I will fetch the tails AND give you
some money when we reach the other side!"

Crocodile wondered
what he might spend his money on...

RESERVED
EVERY NIGHT

MENU
Monkey
Tails

Jungle
Juice

By now, Crocodile was getting very close
to the opposite bank, and was looking forward
to a supper of delicious monkey tails.

"We are nearly there, dear Monkey!
Please could you fetch the tails straight away,
for I am rather hungry?" asked Crocodile.

The crocodile swam the last few strokes
and waded slowly out of the water.

Ameerah Monkey gave a great sigh of relief.
"Yes, yes. Wait there," she shouted.
"I'll be back right away!"

Quick as a flash, she jumped off the crocodile's neck,
and clambered up the nearest tree.

Safe from his big jaws and sharp teeth, she shouted down:
"Stupid, silly Mr Crocodile! How could I leave my tail,
my brother's tail, my sister's tail, my mother's tail
and my father's tail all hanging on the washing line?
Everyone knows you can't take off your tail!

My magic belt will now before your very eyes,
turn into a MONKEY'S TAIL! Here it is! Ta Da!" she cried.
Then, she untied the 'belt' and waved her tail at the bewildered
crocodile, before running off into the trees to explore.

Crocodile had been tricked. There was no bank,
no money, and above all, no delicious monkey tails!
That was all a big bunch of MONKEY BUSINESS!
His tummy rumbled. How could he make that naughty
monkey feel sorry for him? A big round tear began
to trickle down his scaly skin.

"Come back Monkey!" he cried. "I promise I won't eat you!"
he lied, as more false tears trickled down his face....

But Ameerah Monkey was wiser than that.
She knew that you can never trust a crocodile's tears....

And Ameerah Monkey kept her long tail,
her mother and father, sisters and brothers
all kept their long tails - and that is
the happy end of this very long tale!